BiG WoLF
and Little Wolf

BY SHARON PHILLIPS DENSLOW

ILLUSTRATED BY CATHIE FELSTEAD

Greenwillow Books
An Imprint of HarperCollinsPublishers

This one's for Mama,
who used to tell me stories
and sing songs forever until I went
to sleep—S. P. D.

For Beryl and Dudley,
with love—C. F.

Pen and ink and watercolors were used for the full-color art.
The text type is Gill Sans.
Big Wolf and Little Wolf
Text copyright © 2000 by Sharon Phillips Denslow
Illustrations copyright © 2000 by Cathie Felstead
Printed in Singapore by Tien Wah Press. All right reserved.
www.harperchildrens.com

Library of Congress Cataloging-in-Publication Data
Denslow, Sharon Phillips.
Big Wolf and Little Wolf / by Sharon Phillips Denslow ;
pictures by Cathie Felstead.
p.   cm.
"Greenwillow Books."
Summary: Gray wolf father and son sing to each other one night
before being startled by noises in the bushes.
ISBN 0-688-16174-X (trade).   ISBN 0-688-16175-8 (lib. bdg.)
[1. Wolves—Fiction.   2. Parent and child—Fiction.]   I. Felstead, Cathie, ill.
II. Title.   PZ7.D433Bi   2000   [E]—dc21   99-11712   CIP

2 3 4 5 6 7 8 9 10   First Edition

Late one night, just before the moon disappeared,
Big Wolf sat Little Wolf on his knee.

"Sing me a good-night song, Daddy," Little Wolf said.

So Big Wolf sang,

"Oh, a Little Wolf sat on a Big Wolf's knee.

Said the Little Wolf, 'Sing a song for me.'

The Big Wolf stretched his throat out long

and sang Little Wolf this yowly song."

"I'm a wolf. I'm a wolf. I'm a big gray wolf.

I sleep all day, I sing all night,

I snap my teeth in an overbite!

I'm a wolf. I'm a wolf. I'm a big gray wolf.

I like to chew, I like to eat,

I use my nose to smell my feet."

Little Wolf giggled and said, "Sing more, Daddy."

So Big Wolf did.

"I'm a wolf. I'm a wolf. I'm a big gray wolf.

I dig up holes, I scratch up dirt,

I howl at the moon in my old nightshirt!"

"I'm a wolf. I'm a wolf. I'm a big gray wolf.

I chase wild ducks, I jump on bugs,

I wrestle my son and give him hugs."

Little Wolf gave Big Wolf a hug, too.

Then he said, "Here's a song for you, Daddy!"

"I'm a wolf. I'm a wolf. I'm a little gray wolf.

I like to bounce, I like to play,

I chase my tail round and round all day!"

there was a rustling and a growling

in the bushes behind them.

"I hear something, Daddy," said Little Wolf.

"So do I," said Big Wolf.

Then ...

there was a scritching and scratching

in the bushes behind them.

"I hear a scritching and scratching," said Little Wolf.

"So do I," said Big Wolf.

"Who's there?"
Big Wolf growled.

Little Wolf saw two tall ears rise above the bushes.

He saw two big eyes and a big shiny nose, and then he heard . . .

"I'm a wolf. I'm a wolf. I'm a Big Mama Wolf.

I scare silly wolves, I make them run,

I hide in the woods just having fun!"

Big Wolf and Little Wolf yowled
and ran through the bushes
chasing Mama Wolf . . .

until they all fell down in a happy tumble

right in front of their den.

"You almost scared me, Mama!" said Little Wolf.

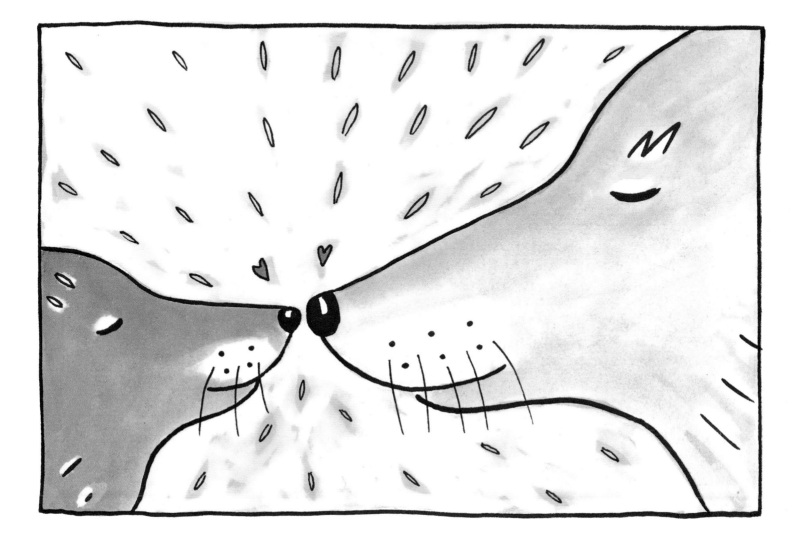

Mama Wolf kissed his nose.

"It's time for bed, Little Wolf," she said.

"But first, sing me a good-night song,"
said Little Wolf.

So Mama Wolf and Big Wolf did.

"We are wolves. We are wolves.

We are fine gray wolves.

Our sleep is deep,

our snores are long,

and in our dreams

there is one more song."

AARROOOO!

ARRROOOOOOOOOO!

AAARRROOOOOOOOOOOOO!

Good night!

PIRATES, HO!

by SARAH L. THOMSON

illustrated by STEPHEN GILPIN

Marshall Cavendish Children

Marshall Cavendish Corporation, 99 White Plains Road, Tarrytown, NY 10591
www.marshallcavendish.us/kids

Library of Congress Cataloging-in-Publication Data
Thomson, Sarah L.
Pirates, ho! / by Sarah L. Thomson ; illustrated by Stephen Gilpin. — 1st ed.
p. cm.
Summary: Pirates Peg-Leg Tom, Angus Black, Dreadful Nell, and One-Eyed Jack chase ships on the
high seas, tell ghost stories, and fall asleep counting gold instead of sheep.
ISBN 978-0-7614-5435-9
[1. Pirates—Fiction. 2. Stories in rhyme.] I. Gilpin, Stephen, ill. II.
Title.
PZ8.3.T3274Pi 2008
[E]—dc22
2007029792

The illustrations are hand-drawn and colored in Adobe Photoshop.
Book design by Anahid Hamparian
Editor: Robin Benjamin

Printed in Malaysia
First edition
1 3 5 6 4 2

To Jack, Julian, Lily, and Grady,
the pirates of Bustins Island
—S.L.T.

For Amos, my fierce little guy
—S.G.

We are pirates, ho! We are tough and mean, the scurviest lot you have ever seen.

There's Peg-Leg Tom and Angus Black,
Dreadful Nell and One-Eyed Jack.
A thieving, lying, rascally crew,
the worst you've heard of us is true,
and nobody tells us what to do—
we are pirates, pirates, ho!

So you want to join this cut-throat band?
You must face peril on every hand.
No fainthearts sail these towering waves—
you'd better be strong and bold and brave.

We shout, "Avast!" We cry, "Ahoy!"
The deadliest danger's our greatest joy.
From the first mate down to the cabin boy,
we are pirates, pirates, ho!

The wind is fierce, the rigging snaps,
the timbers shiver till they crack.
No ship can flee. The chase begins!
There is no battle we can't win.

A skull keeps watch from our flag of bones.
Our swords are steel and our hearts are stone
as we send our foes to Davy Jones.
We are pirates, pirates, ho!

We show no mercy and feel no fear—
except when the gloom of night creeps near.
Then pirates talk of sights they've seen,
like a light in the rigging that glows pale green,

or deep and hidden caves where none
survived to tell of dark deeds done
and ghosts guard treasures lost and won
by pirates, pirates, ho!

Now hear of a captain
who sold his soul

for the glitter of jewels
and the gleam of gold.

He sails a ship glimpsed by a few,
with coal-black flags and a skeleton crew.
Its sails have crumbled into dust,
the captain's sword has turned to rust,
but still it's sailing after . . .

As black waves beat on a moonless shore,
we drop the anchor and sail no more,
hidden from shadows, safe in our beds,
with blankets pulled tight over our heads.

We count our gold instead of sheep
while over the softly slumbering deep,
the only ship that sails is sleep.
We are pirates, pirates . . . *ssshhhhh . . .*

We are pirates,

pirates, HO!